THE GOOSE PIMPLE BAY · SAGAS ·

Spike Carbuncle
and the
Truly Enormous Egg

Karen Wallace
Illustrated by Nigel Baines

A & C Black • London

To Master G

First published 2008 by
A & C Black Publishers Ltd
38 Soho Square, London, W1D 3HB

www.acblack.com

Text copyright © 2008 Karen Wallace
Illustrations copyright © 2008 Nigel Baines

ISBN 978-0-7136-7992-2

A CIP catalogue for this book is available from the British Library.

This book is produced using paper that is made from wood
grown in managed, sustainable forests. It is natural, renewable and
recyclable. The logging and manufacturing processes conform
to the environmental regulations of the country of origin.

Printed and bound in Great Britain by MPG Books Limited.

Spike Carbuncle
and the
Truly Enormous Egg

Chapter One

Spike Carbuncle walked through the forest behind the Great Hall at Goose Pimple Bay, whacking the heads off all the flowers with a big, knobbly stick.

Every time a bunch of petals exploded and fell to the ground, he thought of his brother, Whiff Erik. And thinking of his brother, put Spike into a very bad mood.

Whack! *Whack*! *Whack*! Soon the path was covered in petals.

The truth was, Spike Carbuncle was furious. He was the oldest son in his family. *He* should be chief of Goose Pimple Bay. It was only right and it was what he wanted more than anything else in the whole world. Instead, his brother was chief and Whiff Erik was nothing more than a weedy wet who spent his whole time gardening.

And as for his brother's daft wife, Fernsilver. Spike flattened a pretty daisy with the heel of his boot. *She* spent her time breeding goats, and making cheese and pots of sloppy white stuff, which everyone poured over their berries at meal times.

Spike Carbuncle hated cheese. And as for the sloppy white stuff – while all the other Vikings gobbled theirs up, Spike dumped his behind Whiff Erik's chair. He was secretly hoping his brother would slip on it and break his neck, but that hadn't happened yet.

At that moment, Spike's wife, Fangtrude, jumped down from a tree and landed neatly on the ground in front of him.

Fangtrude was part wolverine and not many people liked her. In fact, she was the main reason Spike wasn't chief of Goose Pimple Bay. His mother and father,

Ma Moosejaw and Chief Thunderstruck, hadn't been able to find anything to like about Fangtrude, so they had chosen Whiff Erik and Fernsilver to run things while they were away.

Now, Fangtrude's sharp, bristly face was twitching and her glittering, red eyes shone.

"What's up with you?" asked Spike Carbuncle in a sulky voice.

In reply, Fangtrude threw back her head and howled.

"Stop acting like a wolverine," snapped Spike. "You know I don't like it."

Fangtrude looked down. "Sorry," she said. "It's just—"

"Just what?"

"Just I've seen something." Fangtrude grabbed her husband's hand and led him quickly through the thick forest. "It's very strange…"

9

"So what?" said Spike Carbuncle, rudely. "You see something strange every time you look in the mirror."

"There's no need to be nasty," replied Fangtrude, resisting the urge to bite him. "The thing is, I've found something that might make you become chief of Goose Pimple Bay."

Spike's eyes lit up. "What is it?"

"Something amazing!" Fangtrude paused and her snout-like nose twitched. "And I have a funny feeling about it."

Spike felt a shiver of excitement rush through his body. "What a sweet, clever furry thing, you are," he said in a gooey voice and squeezed his wife's arm. "Show me what you've seen."

This time, Fangtrude turned and bit him. There was nothing she hated more than someone pretending to say nice things just so they could get what they wanted.

"Cut the soppy stuff," she snarled, and pulled him through a gap in the trees. The next minute, they were standing in a bright, sunny meadow of soft grass and flowers. "Here we are. Now, what do you think about *that*?"

Spike looked around him. He didn't see anything strange, apart from a big pile of hay. He started to feel angry again. It was probably something to do with Fernsilver and her stupid goats. He pulled out his sword, ready to smash the hay into little pieces.

"Stop!" cried Fangtrude. She grabbed Spike's hair. "Can't you see? There's an egg under that straw. A truly enormous egg!"

Thin wisps of smoke were rising from the hay and Spike Carbuncle's stomach rumbled. If it was an egg, it must be cooked by now. He turned to his wife. "Did you bring any salt with you? I hate eggs without salt."

Fangtrude stared at him as if he was crazy. "What on earth are you talking about?" She pointed to the huge pile of straw. "It's not something to eat. It's a *dragon's* egg!"

Chapter Two

Spike Carbuncle stared at the fine wisps of smoke and frowned. If the egg was the same size as the mountain of hay, it must be really huge. And that meant that the dragon inside would be just as big. Slowly, he began to understand why Fangtrude was so excited.

Whiff Erik had brought back a little, fire-breathing dragon from one of his plant-collecting expeditions. He fed it on chillies and, in return, it kept the Great Hall warm.

Now, this enormous dragon's egg was about to hatch into an even bigger

dragon. And it was still only a baby…
Soon this dragon would be gigantic and
terrify the little, fire-breathing dragon and
all the other Vikings, especially Whiff Erik
and Fernsilver.

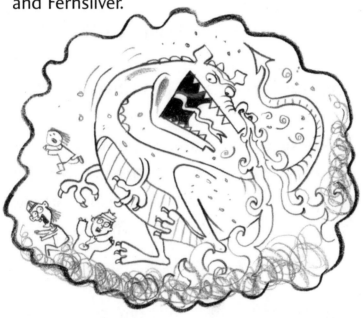

Fangtrude watched the look in Spike
Carbuncle's face change as he finally
worked things out. She grinned her
bristly, sharp-toothed grin. "Got it?"
she asked.

Spike Carbuncle grinned because he had thought of something else. "If we train this dragon to do what we want, then all the other Vikings will have to do what we want, too."

"Exactly," replied Fangtrude. "No one is gong to argue with a fire-breathing monster. And that is just what we'll train him to be."

Spike peered at the pile of hay and now he felt more and more excited. This really could be his chance to get his dearest

wish. Finally, he might become chief of Goose Pimple Bay!

"Are you absolutely sure it's a dragon's egg?" he asked. "I mean, I can see it's big, but how can you be sure?"

Fangtrude crept forward and pushed aside a handful of hay to show a patch of bright-red eggshell. "Dragon eggs are always this colour."

She put her ear to the shell and smiled. "Just as I thought," she said. "It will hatch out at full moon tonight."

✳✳✳

"There's something funny about Spike Carbuncle and Fangtrude," said Fernsilver that night as she lay in bed, drawing pictures of different-shaped cheeses in the special book she kept about her goats. It was a cross between a diary and a record book, and every night she wrote or drew something in it.

"What do you mean 'funny'?" asked Whiff Erik, who was drawing pictures in his own book, which was all about vegetable gardens.

He had just grown 24 rows of huge, spicy onions and he wanted to remember what they looked like before he picked them.

"They are happy," said Fernsilver, shutting her book and blowing out the candle. "And they are whispering all the time."

"Happy? That *does* sound unusual." Whiff Erik shut his own book. "But maybe we're being too suspicious, dear one. Everyone is allowed to be happy."

"Not Fangtrude and Spike Carbuncle," muttered Fernsilver as she turned over and pulled the fur covers up to her chin. "They're up to something, for sure. I think you should keep an eye on them."

Whiff Erik sighed wearily. If only he could have had a nice brother, or at least one that wasn't as mean and horrible as Spike Carbuncle. All he did was cause trouble. Whiff Erik tossed and turned and tried to think of rows and rows of lovely spicy onions instead of his brother's nasty face.

It wasn't easy, but at last he managed to push the thought of Spike Carbuncle from his mind and fell asleep.

✳✳✳

It was midnight and the moon was almost full as Fangtrude and Spike Carbuncle made their way through the trees to the meadow. Spike would never have got there by himself but Fangtrude, being part wolverine, could see in the dark.

As they crossed the meadow, the moon went completely round like a huge, silver plate and suddenly the mountain of hay began to tremble.

"Quick! Get down behind that old tree trunk," whispered Fangtrude, pointing to where a huge log lay on the ground. "We don't want to get hit by bits of flying eggshell."

A minute later, both Fangtrude and Spike Carbuncle watched in amazement as lumps of blackened hay fell to the ground and the enormous egg began to roll about on the grass. Then there was a great crack and a jagged, orange saw appeared out of the broken shell. Eyes blinked in the light of the moon and slowly the dragon scrambled out.

"Tchh!" muttered Fangtrude, clicking her tongue. "That's a pity."

"What's a pity?" asked Spike. Even as a baby, the dragon was ten times the size of the one in the Great Hall.

"He's got green eyes," said Fangtrude. "The red-eyed ones are fiercer."

Spike Carbuncle laughed nastily. "Don't worry, dearest, he'll be fierce by the time we've finished training him." He swung a lumpy sack onto the top of the log. "Do you think he likes onions?"

"Of course. Dragons will eat anything," said Fangtrude, pulling out a bag of hot chillies that she had stolen from Whiff Erik's garden. "Look what I've brought!"

Half an hour later, the baby dragon had happily eaten all the onions and the chillies, but he was still hungry.

"*Now* what are we going to do?" asked Spike Carbuncle.

Fangtrude stood up. "I'll go and get some more vegetables. You stay here and sing to him."

"Don't be daft," snapped Spike Carbuncle. "I'm not singing to a stupid dragon!"

"Shhh!" hissed Fangtrude, kicking him in the shins. "Do as you're told. *I'm* the one that can see in the dark so *I* have to get the vegetables." She peered into Spike Carbuncle's face. "Do you want to be chief of Goose Pimple Bay, or not?"

"Of course I do," muttered Spike.

"Then *sing*," said Fangtrude. "We've got to make this dragon love us."

"I don't understand," said Spike, who had never felt love for anyone or anything. Love was something soppy for weedy wets like his brother. He looked at the green-eyed dragon nervously. "What good will singing do?"

"All babies love being sung to," explained Fangtrude. "And if we make the dragon happy, he'll do what we say." Then she ran off across the meadow with the empty sack in her hands.

Not long after, the dragon began to twitch restlessly and reached out a claw. Spike was just about to push him away when he remembered Fangtrude's orders. He took a deep breath, patted the dragon's claw and began to make a noise that was somewhere between a croak and a gargle.

The baby dragon yawned and put his warm, leathery head in Spike Carbuncle's lap. There was a faint smell of burning tunic, but Spike gritted his teeth and didn't move. The next moment, the dragon was asleep.

Chapter Three

Two days later, Whiff Erik stood looking at his onion patch. He had finished a hard day's gardening and the sun was setting.

Whiff Erik wasn't very good at adding up but he knew he had planted 24 rows of huge, spicy onions because he had written it down in his book and he had even drawn a picture.

He counted on his fingers again. Four rows were missing. Also a dozen chilli plants had disappeared just when the shiny, red chillies were ready for picking. It was a complete mystery.

At first, Whiff Erik wondered if it was Fernsilver. Perhaps she was trying out different flavours for her sloppy white stuff. He imagined it would taste just as good with chopped onions and chillies on top of reindeer nuggets as it did with sugar on top of berries. But Whiff Erik knew Fernsilver would never pick anything from his vegetable garden without asking.

As he turned to go back to the Great Hall, Whiff Erik saw something move on the edge of the field. He ducked behind a tree and watched in stunned silence as Fangtrude appeared from under a bush and began to pull handfuls of his beautiful onions out of the ground and stuff them into a big sack.

Whiff Erik opened his mouth to shout but then shut it again. Fernsilver *had* been right. Spike and Fangtrude were definitely up to something. But what? And why on earth would they need his onions and chillies?

For one wild moment, Whiff Erik wondered if they were preparing to leave Goose Pimple Bay and were taking food for the journey. But he knew it was too much to hope for. Spike hated vegetables and Fangtrude mostly gnawed leftover bones. And anyway, after his last adventure, Spike had sworn he would never leave Goose Pimple Bay again.

Whiff Erik ran back to the Great Hall. He had to find Fernsilver! She would know what to do!

***

"*How* many onions?" cried Fernsilver when Whiff Erik had finished telling her the story.

"Five rows in two days," replied Whiff Erik.

Fernsilver frowned. "I told you to keep an eye on them," she said crossly.

Whiff Erik shrugged. "I've tried, but I haven't noticed anything special. It was just today when I went to the onion patch," he said unhappily.

"Never mind," said Fernsilver. "We're on the case now." She thought hard. "They could be planning something really terrible. You know how much Spike wants to be chief."

Whiff Erik nodded. Sometimes he wished he'd never rescued Spike and brought him back to Goose Pimple Bay after he'd run away from Fangtrude's island.

Fernsilver didn't have to ask what Whiff Erik was thinking. She could tell by the look on his face. "From now on we won't let them out of our sight," she said. "If they go anywhere, we'll follow them. Whatever they're up to, we'll find out and stop them!"

***

At lunch, Spike Carbuncle drank more beer than usual and when Fernsilver put down the pot of sloppy white stuff for pudding, he picked it up and poured it over Whiff Erik's head.

"There you are, dumb brain," shouted Spike Carbuncle. "Now the outside of your head looks just like the inside." He paused and swallowed his beer in a gulp. "One big mess of goop!"

34

All the other Vikings looked at each other uneasily. Apart from the fact that they liked the sloppy white stuff and now Spike had wasted it, there was something different about him. It was almost as if he knew something they didn't and couldn't resist showing off. Even Axehead, who was Spike's best friend, looked unhappy and stared at his empty plate.

Spike drank two more mugs of beer and stood up on his chair. "You wait, you lot," he said in an important voice. "When I'm—"

But he never finished his sentence because Fangtrude had grabbed his foot, and he was flying out of the Great Hall.

"You stupid idiot," she hissed when they were outside. "If you start talking like that, everyone is going to get suspicious."

"So what?" snarled Spike Carbuncle, rubbing his head where it had hit the stone floor with a terrible thud. "We've got the dragon. There's nothing they can do to stop us."

"He's not trained yet," snapped Fangtrude. "Our plan won't work if he doesn't do as he's told."

Spike's eyes lit up. "Why not try him with a tasty goat?"

Fangtrude scratched her bristly snout. "Maybe you're right. OK. We'll steal a couple of Fernsilver's goats and see if he likes them."

"Told you," muttered Spike. "I'm not as stupid as you think."

Back in the Great Hall, Fernsilver nudged Whiff Erik under the table. "Look at the little dragon," she whispered.

Whiff Erik saw that the little dragon was standing as still as a statue. Its green eyes were blazing and every scale on its tail was standing on end. It was staring at the door Spike and Fangtrude had left open, and it was growling.

Fernsilver stood up and pushed away her wooden bowl. It was a signal that lunch was over.

"Hurry," she said, grabbing Whiff Erik by the hand. "Don't let Fangtrude and Spike disappear. We must find out where they're going."

But when they ran out of the door, there was nobody in sight.

Chapter Four

"Are you certain they went this way?" Whiff Erik was following Fernsilver through the forest. Not only was Fernsilver really good at looking after goats, she was also a brilliant tracker.

"Positive," said Fernsilver. She pointed to where there were fresh tracks in the soft ground. "Look! That one with the claw marks is Fangtrude. The one that looks like an elephant is Spike and these two... These two look like *goats* to me!" Fernsilver's eyes blazed. "If anything happens to my goats," she said in a furious voice. "I will—"

"Nothing's going to happen to your goats, dear," interrupted Whiff Erik quickly. He had never seen his wife look so frightening. "Let's hurry. Spike and Fangtrude can't be far away."

Sure enough, Fernsilver led them through a gap in the trees and the next moment, they were standing at the edge of a meadow, staring in complete astonishment.

On one side of the grass was an enormous dragon. On the other side was a huge round target. Behind it, Fangtrude and Spike stood beside a sack of onions. Two goats sat on either side of the dragon as if they were keeping him company.

"Why didn't he eat the goats?" shouted Spike Carbuncle. "Is he some kind of sissy?"

"I told you. He's got green eyes," replied Fangtrude. "He's not a fierce kind of dragon."

"But can we still teach him to breathe fire when he's told to?" asked Spike.

"I think so," said Fangtrude. "Watch! He's getting better." She held up an onion and waved it in front of the dragon. Then she pointed to the middle of the target board. "Burn bull's-eye!" ordered Fangtrude.

A tongue of flame shot out of the dragon's mouth, burnt a wiggly line in the field and sputtered out just before it reached the target.

"NO ONION!" yelled Fangtrude.

The dragon took a deep breath and tried again. This time the flame hit the edge of the

target and knocked it over.

"NO ONION!" yelled Fangtrude again.

Then, to Fernsilver's amazement, the dragon let out a heartbroken howl, lay down on the ground and stuck all four legs in the air. The two goats immediately lay down beside him.

"He must be a nice, kind dragon," whispered Fernsilver to Whiff Erik. "Otherwise my goats wouldn't like him."

Spike Carbuncle was furious. "It's no good," he snarled. "How can I force Whiff Erik out of Goose Pimple Bay if this stupid dragon can't throw his fire straight?"

"So *that's* what he's up to," hissed Fernsilver. "He's got a nerve. Well, he's not going to get away with it."

In the middle of the meadow, Fangtrude marched towards the dragon and whispered in his ear. "Get it right or you're for the chop!"

The poor dragon didn't need to be told twice. He jumped to his feet, trembling all over. Then he shot a bolt of fire straight into the centre of the target.

45

"That's better," said Fangtrude in a nasty, sing-song voice.

Fernsilver took Whiff Erik's hand. "Let's go home," she whispered. "We've seen enough. Now we need to make a plan – fast."

❋❋❋

Back at the Great Hall, Fernsilver thought hard. "We've got to find a way of forcing their hand," she said at last.

Whiff Erik spread his fingers as far apart as possible and forced them back together. No ideas came to him. "What do you mean?" he asked.

"Somehow we have to make Spike and Fangtrude put their plan into action and bring the dragon to the Great Hall."

"How about a barbecue?" suggested Whiff Erik. "Spike loves barbecues and it would be just the chance he's looking for to show off his dragon."

"Brilliant!" cried Fernsilver. She grinned. "We'll have a barbecue to celebrate your first year as chief of Goose Pimple Bay. That should drive them both crazy!"

Whiff Erik gave his wife a big kiss. "Fernsilver!" he said. "You're a genius!"

✳✳✳

"A what?" shouted Spike Carbuncle, his face black with rage.

"A barbecue," said Axehead. He pulled out a piece of animal skin with writing on it. It said:

BARBECUE

TOMORROW NIGHT

Everyone is invited.

(Come in fancy dress)

"Why's Whiff Erik having a barbecue?" snarled Spike.

"Because he's been chief for a year," said Axehead. "It's a celebration."

"We'll make it a celebration all right," snarled Fangtrude when Axehead had gone. She turned to Spike Carbuncle.

"Can't you see? This is our chance to bring the dragon to the Great Hall and get rid of Whiff Erik for good! By the end of the day, *we're* going to be the ones who are celebrating, not him!"

Chapter Five

The next night, all the Vikings took their places at the long table. The walls of the Great Hall had been decorated with flowers and vegetables in honour of Whiff Erik. And the little, fire-breathing dragon had been given a collar of red and orange jewels especially for the occasion.

Everyone was wearing wonderful clothes because Vikings love fancy-dress more than anything in the whole world. Even Axehead had put on the specially embroidered cape his mother had made

him and a headdress stuck with eagle feathers.

"Vikings of Goose Pimple Bay!" Fernsilver cried, raising her mug in the air. "We are here to celebrate our great chief, Whiff Erik, who has looked after us all brilliantly for one whole year!"

As she spoke, Whiff Erik was lowered down from the ceiling, sitting on a great wooden throne with four ropes at each corner. He was dressed in a purple cloak and was wearing the helmet with the horns, which was only brought out for battles and special occasions. Poor Whiff Erik! He had never been so embarrassed in his life. But Fernsilver had insisted.

"We have to drive Spike and Fangtrude crazy with jealousy," she had said earlier that evening. "It's the only way we can guarantee they'll bring the dragon."

Sure enough, as all the other Vikings cheered when they saw Whiff Erik on his throne, Spike Carbuncle roared with rage and yanked open the double doors.

Fangtrude gave a low, piercing whistle and the next minute, a large, green-eyed dragon stomped into the room, its red-hot nostrils aimed straight at Whiff Erik.

A great gasp went around as Spike
Carbuncle jumped on to his chair. "Vikings
of Goose Pimple Bay," he began. "The
time has come—"

Then something extraordinary
happened. The little, fire-breathing
dragon ran forward and looked at the
big dragon.

They both had green eyes.

The little dragon made a soft, mewing
sound and the big one mewed back. The
next moment the big dragon's red-hot

nostrils turned blue and he lay down on the floor. The little, fire-breathing dragon jumped from the table and sat down beside him.

No one spoke. You could have heard a cricket cough.

"Well," said Fernsilver, fixing Spike Carbuncle with her clear, blue eyes. "What time has come?"

Spike Carbuncle fiddled with his sword and stared hopelessly at Fangtrude. *Now* what was he supposed to do?

"This was your idea in the first place," he muttered in Fangtrude's hairy ear, as he climbed down from his chair.

"Well?" said Fernsilver again. "Surely you must have a reason for bringing a huge, fire-breathing dragon into the Great Hall?"

Fangtrude knew it was up to her. Spike was too stupid to think up an excuse on the spot. "Of course, we had a reason!" she cried. "Spike and I were walking through the meadow one day, picking flowers for our house when we saw this enormous dragon's egg."

"*You* saw it," snarled Spike Carbuncle. "*I* wanted to eat it, if you remember."

At this, the big dragon lifted his head and narrowed his eyes suspiciously.

"And anyway," said Fangtrude, looking nervously at the dragon. "We thought, oh, how wonderful, we will hatch the egg and take the big dragon to the Great Hall and give him to Whiff Erik. Then he can help the little dragon keep everyone warm when the winter comes."

"That was my idea," said Spike, who was determined to make himself look like as nice as possible. "I always like to think about other people."

The big dragon got on his feet and made a furious growling noise. He had heard enough. He picked up Spike Carbuncle and Fangtrude in one claw, and everyone watched in horror as his nostrils began to turn bright red again.

"No!" said Fernsilver firmly. "Put them down! We do not set anyone on fire in Goose Pimple Bay, no matter what they've done."

The big dragon looked from Fernsilver to the little dragon, who solemnly shook his head and pointed to the door.

The next moment, the big dragon stomped outside with Spike Carbuncle and Fangrude still dangling from his claw. He dropped them on the ground and, just to show he meant business, he blew a great burst of flame by their feet, which made them run into the forest, howling and hopping at the same time.

"Enough!" cried Whiff Erik, getting up from his great wooden throne. "This is my barbecue and I'm hungry! Let's eat!"

And so it happened that the little dragon and the big dragon cooked supper for all the Vikings that night. There were roasted reindeer nuggets, all kinds of vegetables and, for pudding, extra-large helpings of berries and sloppy white stuff. It was the most fantastic celebration barbecue ever.

And they all agreed that the absolutely best thing about it was that Spike Carbuncle and Fangtrude were not there!

Chief Thunderstruck and the Big Bad Bear

"Jump! Jump for your life!"

Chief Thunderstruck is in trouble. He's been snatched from his wife by a big, bad bear. Then Spike Carbuncle finds a message in a bottle. It's from his mother and says **HELP!** Immediately, Spike and his brother, Whiff Erik, set off on a rescue mission. But will they get there before the bear eats Chief Thunderstruck for breakfast? Only a certain wolverine knows what to do...

The fourth hilarious adventure in The Goose Pimple Bay Sagas

Available Now!